# Gorilla Gardener

How to Help NATuRE Take Over the World

BY

JOHN & JANA

Manic D

San Francisco

Also by
John & Jana

A Rule is to Break:
A Child's Guide to Anarchy
&
Happy Punks 1 2 3

Gorilla Gardener ©2017 by John Seven & Jana Christy
All rights reserved. ISBN 978-1-945665-00-4
Published by Manic D Press. For information, contact
Manic D Press, PO Box 410804, San Francisco CA 94141
www.manicdpress.com
Printed in the USA          CPSAI compliant

Gorilla Gardener has a plan.

It's a very simple plan.

# STEP ONE:
# GET SOME SEEDS

Surprise!
I'm a seed!

You can collect them from food or flowers or buy them in packets!

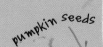

pumpkin seeds

I'm making seed bombs! They're fun to toss!

Stick them in your pocket. Or maybe carry a bag of them. Make sure they're not too heavy!

Just combine clay, seeds, dirt, and water and form into a ball!

# STEP TWO: PLANT SEEDS

Hi!

GoriLLa Gardener pLants them in pLaygrounds and parking Lots,

ON SIDEWALKS
⁑AND⁑
TELEPHONE POLES

And sticks the seeds in EVERY crack EVERY-WHERE!

GoriLLa Gardener swings on wires and pLants seeds on the sides of buiLdings.

They are pLaced in the cracks of bricks and concrete and even thrown onto rooftops!

# STEP THREE: WATCH THE PLANTS GROW

Flowers and berries sprout up from the cracks in the sidewalk

and beans climb up telephone poles and buildings. Squash and pumpkins creep everywhere.

I love gravity!
GET OUTSIDE and LEARN SOMETHING in the SUNSHINE!

If you ever feel like munching on a carrot or a kumquat, keep your eyes peeled!

And strawberries and tomatoes
and pLenty more to eat, too!

# WHO CAN WORK WITH ALL THIS CLUTTER IN THE OFFICE?

Kids and animals sure make a racket together!

Grown-ups have to go outside!
Maybe they will act a little wild, too!

VINES SPILL FROM

GoriLLa
Gardener
has something
new to
swing on!

SCRAPERS

IVY CLIMBS UP THE SKY

# THE ROOFS

IT'S FUN TO SLEEP IN TREES LIKE GORILLA GARDENER!

Don't worry, it's just wild boars frolicking in the moonlight.

# SOME GRUMPS WON'T LIKE IT.

Even the butterflies
are happy!

Maybe that grump will join everyone in celebrating the
new wild and free world.
What a feast there will be among the trees and grass!

What else can we see?
Seeds from our city floating in the air on to the next one!
Pretty soon that will be a jungle city, too.
And there will be another one and another one...

Let's thank GoriLLa Gardener,
and pLant even more seeds!

# YOU CAN BE A

Hi! Would you like to start a garden with us?

## How to Harvest Seeds

Each of these flowers, fruits, and vegetables has seeds in OR on it!

Carefully remove the seeds once the flower, fruit, or vegetable has fully ripened and bloomed.

Gently pick off any bits that are stuck to the seeds.

Rinse fruit and vegetable seeds with water and let dry.

If you won't be using your seeds right away, store them in a cool, dry, dark place.

(seeds that are "hybrid" won't work.)

♥ Experiment & Research! ♥

## HOW TO MAKE SEED BOMBS

There are LOTS of ways to make Seed Bombs! Here's one:

Mix Together

1 part wildflower seeds + 1 part compost or rich soil + 5 parts air-dry red clay

(add a few drops of water if necessary to hold it all together.)

Knead everything

then pinch off chunks and roll into balls.

Toss them on to hard to reach spots!

NOW GO!

# GORILLA GARDENER, TOO!

## How to Grow Food From FOOD!

If I stick these in dirt they will grow into new food!

a pineapple top!

garlic cloves!

celery bottom!

a potato that has a little sprout!

a sprouting onion!

Some are pretty easy—like potatoes, garlic and onions.

SoMe are a WEE bit trickier, Like CeLery and PineappLe.

Celery likes to spend its first week in a saucer with some water, then plop it into dirt!

If you live in a part of the world with COLD winters, you'll need to grow pineapples inside in a pot!

It makes me happy to watch things grow!

♥ Learn & GROW! ♥

LOOK! New great food!

One potato turned into SO MANY potatoes!

Remember that all plants need sunshine, water and Patience.

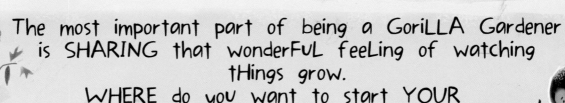

Free Beans!

The most important part of being a GoriLLA Gardener is SHARING that wonderFuL feeLing of watching tHings grow.
WHERE do you want to start YOUR
GORiLLA GARDEN?

Visit www.johnandjana.com for more information about GoriLLa Gardening and internet Links!

# THE HISTORY OF GUERILLA GARDENING

The first guerrilla gardeners were a group in England in the 1600s called the Diggers. At that time, England was in disarray with civil war. Different groups of citizens fought to determine what kind of government the country would have. The Diggers believed in equality and religious freedom, advocated for a parliamentary style that represented the people, and encouraged farming on unused public land as part of their political efforts.

The first act of guerrilla gardening ever was in April 1649 when the Diggers planted vegetables and camped on St. George's Hill in the town of Weybridge. They were run out of town months later, following violence and a court case, but the Diggers and their ideas spread out to many other towns in England to further their cause.

One of the most famous guerrilla gardeners was Johnny Appleseed, an early conservationist who roamed America in the 19th century. Born John Chapman, he used frontier laws to build apple tree nurseries on unclaimed land across the country. Guerrilla gardening made a comeback in the 1960s, with groups like the Green Guerrillas creating community gardens on public land that you can still visit today, like the Liz Christy Garden in New York City and People's Park in Berkeley, CA.

There are now guerrilla gardening movements all over the world- in the United States, England, Scotland, Italy, France, The Netherlands, Belgium, and more. You can go online to connect with them, make guerrilla gardening friends, and get guidance for your own guerrilla gardening efforts.

## NOW LET'S GET OUT THERE AND TOSS SOME SEEDS!